Alexander McCall Smith
Precious
and the
Zebra Necklace

First published in Great Britain in 2015 by
Birlinn Ltd
West Newington House
10 Newington Road
Edinburgh EH9 1QS

www.birlinn.co.uk

ISBN 978 1 78027 327 3
eBook ISBN 978 0 85790 806 3
Text copyright © Alexander McCall Smith 2015
Illustration and design copyright © Iain McIntosh
2015

A CIP catalogue record for this book is available
from the British Library.

Printed and bound in Italy by
Grafica Veneta S.P.A.

Alexander McCall Smith

Precious

and the

Zebra Necklace

Illustrated by
Iain McIntosh

BC

This is for
Douglas Richard Mant

AFRICA

Botswana

THIS IS THE STORY of a girl who was a private detective. Now, you may ask, what is a private detective? Well, a private detective is a person who solves mysteries for other people. So if you or I have something we really want to find out about – maybe a secret of some sort – then we may well ask a private detective to help. That's what they do. Private detectives are very good at finding out things. They look for clues. They ask all sorts of questions. They know just who did what, and when they did it.

1

This is a picture of a typical private detective, but here is a picture of a rather special private detective. Can you spot the difference? Well done! (And that shows that you might be a bit of a private detective yourself!) One is a woman, and the other is ... a girl.

Precious started to be a private detective when she was only nine, which is how old she was when all this happened. She was just an ordinary girl, who went to school like everybody else, and who had to remember to do her homework and so on. But in her spare time she solved mysteries, and sorted out problems for other people. She enjoyed doing this, as she was good at it, you see, and if you are good at something, then doing it is always fun.

"I like solving mysteries," Precious said to her friends. "And the more mysterious they are, the better!"

This mystery was one of those very mysterious ones, and it all started, as many such mysteries do, in an ordinary way. This is what happened.

Precious lived in Botswana, a country in Africa, and her school was at the top of a hill. Every morning the children lined up outside the classroom before going in for the start of their lessons. To help the teachers count the pupils, everyone in the line called out a number in turn, starting with number 1 and ending with ... Well, they usually ended with number 30, but on this particular morning the last number to be called out was 31. There was a new member of the class, a girl, and her name was Nancy.

"This is your new friend Nancy," announced the teacher once the children had streamed into the classroom. "And now we must find somewhere for her to sit."

Her gaze fell on Precious and the teacher's mind was made up. Precious was a kind girl, and the teacher knew that she would be helpful to somebody who was just starting at a new school.

"Sit over there," she said to Nancy. "You'll look after her, won't you, Precious?"

Precious nodded. She liked the look of the new girl, who had a very friendly smile on her face. Here is a picture of it.

A person who has a smile like that, thought Precious, is bound to be exactly the sort of person you would want as a friend. And that is just what happened. After no more than ten minutes, Precious and Nancy were firm friends. After half an hour, it was as if they had known one another all their lives.

That afternoon, when Precious went home after school, she told her aunt about Nancy, and about how she and Nancy had got on so well. This aunt was now living with Precious and her father, as Precious's own mother was no longer alive, and they needed somebody to run the house when Precious's father was away working with his cattle. The aunt was a cheerful woman who never seemed to be in a bad mood and was widely known as one of the best cooks in that part of Botswana.

She was also quite good at fixing cars, and at one time or another she had fixed the cars of many of their neighbours. She knew everything – not just how brakes and gearboxes worked, but also about people. That was because everybody was happy to talk to her. There are some people like that, as you know: people like to talk to them *because they listen*. This aunt was a very good listener.

Here is a picture of the aunt making a cake ... and here is a picture of her fixing a car. And here is a picture of Precious telling her aunt about the new girl at school, and the aunt is about to turn round and ask, "What did you say her name was, Precious?"

And Precious replied, "She's called

Nancy. And she lives over near the water tower. She pointed the house out to me."

Her aunt nodded. "I know those people," she said. "They have just come here. I forget where they lived before this, but I think it was far away. That little girl has no mother – a bit like you."

"Her mother died?" asked Precious.

The aunt shrugged. "I don't know what happened. But those people have looked after her since she was very small. They are very kind."

That was all that she said about Nancy, and the aunt then went on to talk about a special cake that she was planning to bake. She had been given a large packet of raisins, and raisins were just right for the sort of cake she wanted to make.

Precious agreed. She liked all sorts of cake, but the aunt's cakes were far and away the best she had tasted. Here is a picture of one of them. If you scratch the picture ever so gently with the fingernail of one of your fingers, you may just be able to get the smell of that cake. The smell is not coming from the page, of course – it's coming from inside your head. Can you smell it? I can – and it smells delicious.

Precious thought about Nancy before she dropped off to sleep that night. It is always nice to have a new friend, as having a new friend can give you a warm feeling inside – a feeling made up of excitement and interest and guesses. And yet, when she thought about Nancy, Precious also felt a little bit worried. She thought there was

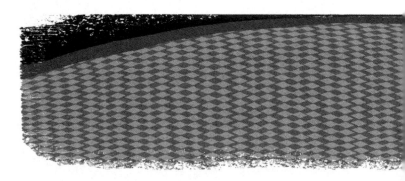

something about Nancy that she was yet
to find out. It was as if her new friend had
some mystery in her life – and Precious had
no idea what that mystery might be.

Well, she thought as she drifted off to
sleep, *I'm sure I will soon find out*. And she
did – the very next day.

I T ALL HAPPENED because of a burst pipe. The children were sitting in their classroom the next morning, working hard on a task their teacher had set them. This was to write a letter – in very neat handwriting – to an imaginary person or a person who was well known. The teacher had shown them how to do it, writing a sample letter on the board in her very beautiful handwriting.

"You start the letter, *Dear*, and then you put in the person's name after that," explained the teacher. "Then you go on to say what you have to say – remembering

13

to be polite, of course – and then you sign
it off with *Yours truly*, and you put your
name after that."

A boy in the front row raised his hand.
"Why do you say *truly*?" he asked.

"It is to show them that you have not
been telling any lies," said the teacher.

"You're saying that it's all true. Any other questions?"

Nobody said anything, as they were keen to get on with practising their own letters. You did not have to know the person you were writing to, said the teacher, as this was really just a practice and the letters would not be sent.

Precious decided that she would write to the President of Botswana, which was the country in Africa where she lived.

"Dear Mr President," she began. And then she stopped to think very hard. What would she want to say to the President of Botswana if she ever had the chance to speak to him? What would any of us say if we were given the chance to speak to somebody as important as that?

She wrote the next sentence. "I would like to ask you about any plans that you have to stop people throwing litter on the ground. Please could you tell me about them. Yours truly, Precious Ramotswe."

She looked at what Nancy was writing. Her friend's letter was to the manager of the television station. Nancy was offering to read the news for them. "You won't have to pay me," she wrote, "as I will do it for nothing. My reading is quite good, and you can even ask my teacher about that if you want to check up."

Precious began to imagine what it would be like to turn on a television set and see one of your friends there. It would be very strange, she decided, although she imagined that you would get used to it after a while.

It was while she was thinking this that the water pipe just outside the classroom burst. It was an important pipe, as it provided the whole school with water, and it was also a large one. This meant that once water started spraying out of the pipe, it soon covered the ground beneath it and then began to flow into the classrooms.

The school handyman did his best to fix the pipe, but the task was beyond him. By now the level of water in the classrooms made it necessary for everybody to raise their feet off the ground, and this was becoming tiring. From her office at the end of the corridor, the principal made her mind up.

"Everybody should go home," she announced. "School is closed for the day."

Everybody was very excited and pleased. "No more school for the rest of the day!" exclaimed Precious, who liked school but also liked the idea of an unexpected holiday.

"Let's go to my house," said Nancy. "It's not far away."

Precious thought this was a very good idea, and soon the two friends were on their way to the house near the water tower.

"What can we do at your place?" asked Precious, as they left the school gate behind them.

Nancy thought for a moment before she replied. "There's something I want to show you," she said.

"What is it?" asked Precious.

Nancy gave her a special sort of smile –
the sort of smile that people give you when
they don't want to say too much just yet.
"You'll soon find out," she said.

"Give me a clue," pressed Precious. "Just
a small clue, and then let me guess."

"Zebra," said Nancy.

Precious hardly knew what to say. She
knew that people had unusual pets, but she
had never heard of anybody who had a zebra.

"You've got a zebra!" she exclaimed.

Nancy laughed. "You'll find out," she said.

Precious spent the rest of the journey wondering how you would look after a pet zebra. What would you feed it on? Was there special striped food for zebras, or did

they just eat grass like horses did? And did zebras bite – as ponies and donkeys sometimes did – or did being stripy make them gentler? And how would you find your zebra if it ran away and hid in the bush, where there were lots of striped shadows? Would you even be able to see him there?

When they arrived at the house, Precious was introduced to the people who looked after Nancy. She called them Aunt and Uncle, and they seemed to Precious to be kind and generous people. You can always tell when somebody is kind, she thought: you look into their eyes and you can see it straight away.

"Tell me all about yourself," said the aunt. "That is, if you don't mind. You don't have to if you don't want to."

Precious smiled; she did not mind at all. And so she told the aunt and the uncle about how she lived with her father. She told them about her own aunts and about the cattle they kept. She told them about the school on the hill and about the fun they all had there.

The aunt made a jug of lemonade for the two girls. It was a hot day and the cold drink was very welcome. But Precious was anxious to see the surprise that Nancy had planned for her.

"Please don't keep me waiting any longer," she pleaded.

Nancy smiled. "All right," she said. "Come into my room and I'll show you."

ANCY LED THE WAY into the small room that she occupied at the back of the house. It had a tiny window, so it was quite dark inside.

"Have you got anything that's really important to you?" she asked Precious.

Precious thought for a moment. She had a dress that an aunt had passed on to her. It was a very special dress, with lines of beads sewn into the hem, and she was keeping it for the day when it would fit her. There was that, and then there was a camera that she had been given for her last birthday. Unfortunately it was broken, but one day

25

somebody might be able to fix it. That was special too.

"I've got a very nice dress," she replied. "And a camera that doesn't quite work."

Nancy nodded. Then she moved across the room to open the door of a small cupboard beside her bed. Very carefully she took out a cloth that had been used to wrap something up. She unfolded this cloth and took out the contents.

"These are my special things," she said. "I love them very much."

Precious looked down. There on her friend's upturned palms was a necklace

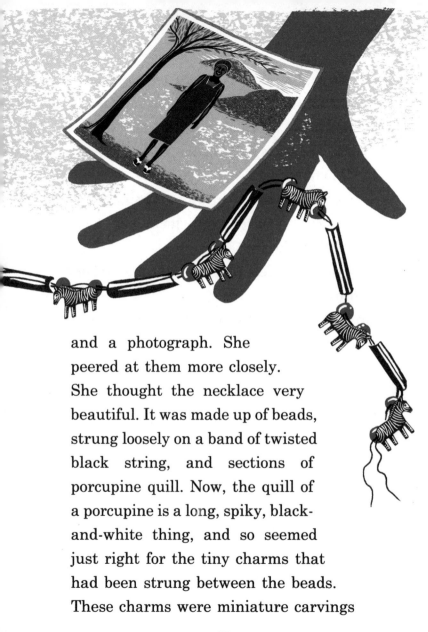

and a photograph. She
peered at them more closely.
She thought the necklace very
beautiful. It was made up of beads,
strung loosely on a band of twisted
black string, and sections of
porcupine quill. Now, the quill of
a porcupine is a long, spiky, black-
and-white thing, and so seemed
just right for the tiny charms that
had been strung between the beads.
These charms were miniature carvings

27

of zebras, made out of bone perhaps, or of stone that had been stained black and white to match the zebra stripes. It was the most beautiful necklace Precious had ever seen.

"Do you like it?" asked Nancy.

Precious nodded. "I think it's wonderful," she said. "You're very lucky to have something like that."

Nancy seemed pleased that her friend approved of her treasure. "Now look at this," she said, passing on to the other item.

It was a photograph of a woman. The photograph was rather old and had become a bit tattered so that it was rather hard to make out the woman's face. She was standing under a tree, and in the background there was a hill, with another small hill behind it in the distance. That was all there was in the photograph.

Precious looked at her friend, enquiringly. "Who is it?" she asked.

"It's my mother," said Nancy, gazing down at the picture of the woman.

Precious said nothing. There was sadness in Nancy's voice, and Precious understood how she must feel.

Nancy sighed. "That's all I have to remind me of her," she said. "I don't even know her name. I was left all alone when I was very small – I don't remember it at all. I had a small bag with me, they say, and in it was the necklace and this photograph. Somebody said that they had belonged to my mother, and that is what I have always believed."

Precious touched the necklace. The zebra charms were smooth and cold on the tips of her fingers. Then she looked at the photograph again. An idea had come to her.

"Will you lend me the photograph?" she asked.

Nancy hesitated. Then she said, "Will you be very careful with it? Promise?"

"Of course I will," said Precious.

"Why do you want to borrow it?" asked Nancy as she handed it to her friend.

The answer surprised her.

"I thought I might try to find out about her for you," said Precious.

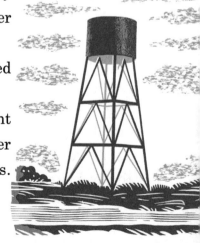

"You see, I'm a bit of a detective, and when there is something that needs to be found out, I like to see if I can help."

Nancy's face broke into a smile. "Will you?" she asked. "Will you find my mother?"

Precious realised that she should not raise the other girl's hopes too much. "I'll do my best," she said. "I can't promise anything, but I shall try."

Nancy handed her the photograph. "Please," she said. "Please do what you can."

At home that evening, Precious showed the photograph to her father. She told him about Nancy and about how the picture and the necklace had been her only possessions when, as a baby, she was taken in by her uncle and aunt. He listened quietly and then, when she had finished the story, he looked very carefully at the photograph.

"This is very interesting," he said. "Yes, this is very interesting indeed."

Precious caught her breath. "Do you know who that lady is?" she asked. She hardly dared hope, but there was always a chance – just a chance – that he might once have met the person in the picture.

He shook his head. "No, I do not know that."

He saw that she was disappointed, and so he continued quickly, "But I do know *where* it was taken."

Precious's eyes widened as she waited for him to tell her.

"It's a very small village on the edge of the

desert," her father went on. "I know those hills, you see. They have a very unusual shape, as you can see in this photo. I went there once as a boy. A cousin of mine lived in that place."

She hardly dared hope. Her voice was quivering with excitement when she spoke. "Does the cousin still live there?"

Her father smiled. "Yes," he said. "She does. She has a farm there. I have seen her cattle when she sends them down here."

Precious asked him to tell her more about the village. "It's a very lonely place," he said. "It's very far from anywhere. Not many people go there."

Precious thought for a moment. Her father had said that not many people went there, but he had not said that *nobody* went there.

"Do you know anybody who might be going there?" she asked.

He scratched his head for a moment.

"Well, as it happens," he said, "I do know a nurse who goes to help in the clinic there quite regularly. She can't drive all the way to the village because the tracks are too narrow and bumpy. But she goes within about four or five miles of it and then walks the rest."

Precious was excited to hear this. "Do you think Nancy and I could go with her?" she said. "We'd be careful."

He looked doubtful. "I don't know, my darling. It's a long way and it's quite wild out there, you know."

"We'd be *very* careful," said Precious. "I promise you."

Obed Ramotswe knew that his daughter was a very responsible girl, and that if she said she would be very careful, then she would be very careful.

"Very well," he said. "You can go. But make sure that Nancy gets permission too."

"I shall," said Precious.

That night as she lay in bed sleep was

slow to come to her. But when it eventually did, she dreamed a lot. She dreamed that she was walking through the bush with Nancy. She dreamed that they were both in some sort of danger. She tossed and turned and eventually woke up. The dream faded quickly, as dreams often do – even bad ones. But she did remember that she had felt very frightened, which is how you usually feel when you are in danger, even if you don't know or can't remember exactly what the danger is.

But it did not put her off. Precious was one of the bravest girls in Botswana, and it would take more than a dream to put her off once she had started working on a case. And so she told Nancy about her plan, and went with her friend to obtain permission to go off on their trip with the nurse.

Nancy was allowed to go, especially since her aunt knew the nurse and knew how careful she would be. So the aunt said yes and made several meals for the girls to take with them. There were sandwiches and cake. There were two cans of orange juice and four apples – two for each girl. Armed with these supplies, and with various other bits and pieces that Precious had gathered together, the two girls, accompanied by Obed Ramotswe, went off to meet the nurse at the crossroads where she said she would pick them up. They were both very excited. This was, in fact, the most exciting thing that Precious Ramotswe had ever done in her entire life.

Obed Ramotswe had some parting words for his daughter and her friend: "When you get there," he said' "make sure you go straight to my cousin's place. She'll be expecting you."

"We shall," said Precious. "Don't worry – we'll be perfectly all right."

Her father stayed with them at the crossroads until the nurse drove up in her car. Then he stood there, waving until the car disappeared into a cloud of dust and was gone.

"Be very careful," he said, as he watched them go. But the wind swallowed his words, and nobody could hear them anyway.

THEY LEFT EARLY in the morning.
The drive took four hours, but
Precious and Nancy both got a
bit of sleep as the car bumped
its way over the rough roads. At last they
reached the place where the road became
a narrow track, and, shortly after that,
turned into an even narrower path.

"We'll leave the car over there," said the
nurse. "That tree will provide some shade
for it."

The girls helped the nurse take her bag
out of the car and the three of them then
began to make their way along the path to

the village. It was obviously not used very much, as it was quite overgrown. In some places it had been more or less washed away by heavy rain; in other places, undergrowth had covered it, making it necessary to pick one's way through dense bush and beds of tall reeds.

They had been walking for half an hour or so, making very slow progress, when Nancy suddenly let out a sharp cry of pain. Precious, who was walking behind her, rushed up to see what had happened.

"A really big thorn," wailed Nancy. "I've trodden on a horrid thorn."

Precious bent down to examine her friend's foot. Sure enough, there was a large thorn, broken off on its shaft, embedded in the sole of Nancy's right foot.

"I'll take it out," said Precious. "You lean on my shoulder, close your eyes, and think of something nice. Think of ice cream."

"What flavour?" Nancy sobbed.

But before an answer could be given,

Precious had pulled the thorn out of the foot. "There we are," she said. "All over."

Nancy was relieved, but wanted to take a short rest. The nurse, who had been walking in front of them, must have been unaware of the incident, and there was now no sign of her.

"We'll catch up with her," said Precious. "We can rest for a few minutes until your foot stops hurting."

The two girls sat down on the ground. All around them were the sounds of the African bush: the high-pitched screech of crickets, the strange, lonely calls of the birds, the sigh of the breeze in the leaves of the trees – a sound that seemed a little like that of the sea.

At last Precious said that it was time to go. She did not want the nurse to get too far ahead of them, because if the nurse turned round and saw that they were not there she

would become alarmed.

"We must hurry," said Precious. "Are you able to walk a little bit faster?"

Nancy replied that she was, and so Precious set off at a rather faster pace than before. This, I'm afraid to say, was a mistake, because the faster you walk in the bush, the more likely you are to lose your way. And that is exactly what happened.

Precious was not sure where they went wrong. It may have been immediately after their rest, when they took what they thought was the right path, or it may have been later on, when they followed the course of a dry river bed. Or it may have been when they wandered into a thick clump of trees and had difficulty finding their way

out again. There are a hundred different ways of getting lost in thick bush like that.

After they had been walking for a while, Precious looked down at the ground. Her father had told her about tracking, and how you can tell who has been there before you by reading what is written in the sand. Now, as she looked down, Precious realised that there were no footprints at all – or at least no footprints of a person, and of the nurse in particular. Nobody had walked that way for a long time – nobody, that is, apart from a warthog and her babies, a

small family of antelopes, and, she thought, a baboon or two.

Nancy knew that something was wrong. "Are we lost?" she asked.

Precious looked up at the sky. It is possible to tell what direction you are going in by looking where the sun is. But now, in this unfamiliar place, it seemed to her that they were going back the way they had come, or were even going round in circles.

She answered Nancy's question carefully. She did not want to alarm her friend. "We might be a little bit lost," she said. "I'm not sure. Perhaps we should try calling the nurse. We may not be too far behind her."

They started to call out. They called as loudly as they could, but their voices did not carry very far in that lonely place. Then they shouted out more loudly, and even tried to whistle, but all that greeted their

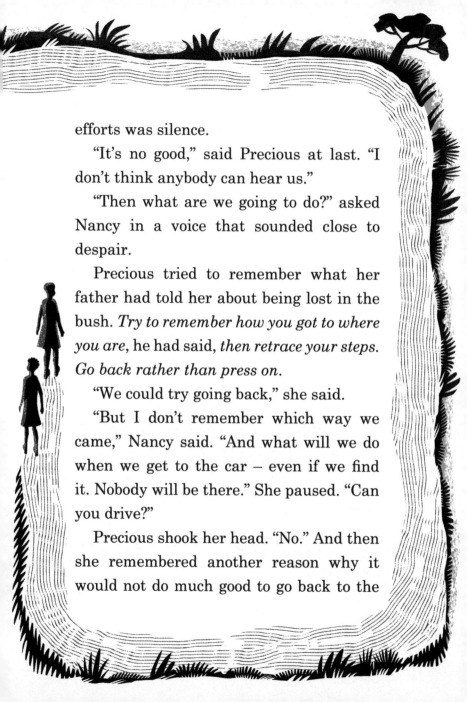

efforts was silence.

"It's no good," said Precious at last. "I don't think anybody can hear us."

"Then what are we going to do?" asked Nancy in a voice that sounded close to despair.

Precious tried to remember what her father had told her about being lost in the bush. *Try to remember how you got to where you are*, he had said, *then retrace your steps. Go back rather than press on.*

"We could try going back," she said.

"But I don't remember which way we came," Nancy said. "And what will we do when we get to the car – even if we find it. Nobody will be there." She paused. "Can you drive?"

Precious shook her head. "No." And then she remembered another reason why it would not do much good to go back to the car. "And we don't have the key," she added. "You need a key to start the engine, and the nurse has taken it with her."

For a few minutes they stood where they were, looking about them, uncertain what to do. It was mid-afternoon now, and in a couple of hours it would be dark. Neither of them wanted to be lost in the African bush at night. It was perfectly possible that there were lions not far away, or leopards perhaps. Leopards like to hunt in the hours

of darkness, and if they were to meet a leopard … It was best not to think about what would happen then.

Eventually Precious made up her mind. "We can try to retrace our tracks," she said. "Then, if we find the path again, we can follow it until we come to the village.

They began to walk back the way they had come. It was slow-going, as the ground was hard and dry, and their footprints were not all that obvious. After half an

hour or so, they came to a halt.

"I can't see any footprints now," said Precious. "Can you see anything, Nancy?"

Nancy had been gazing at the ground in search of some sign, but had found nothing. She shook her head sadly. "I think we're still lost," she said. "Maybe even more lost than we were before."

It was while they were standing there, trying in vain to work out where they were, that Precious heard an unexpected sound. Without saying anything, she reached out to touch Nancy's arm. Then, leaning forward, she whispered in her ear, "I think I heard something. Listen."

The two girls strained their ears. They heard the sound of a bird flying up into a tree – the flutter of wings and a high-pitched bird-call. They heard the rustle of the wind in a reed bed behind them. They heard some tiny sounds that could have been anything – ants, even, marching across tiny grains of sand.

Then they heard something quite different.

"There," said Precious. "Did you hear that?"

Nancy nodded. It seemed very unlikely – so unlikely, in fact, as to be impossible. But there it was again. It was somebody singing.

THERE IT WAS AGAIN. And now it was getting closer.

"Somebody's coming," whispered Nancy.

Precious put a finger to her lips in a gesture of silence. She had worked out that the sound was coming from a thicket of trees not far away. She strained her eyes to see any movement, and then suddenly she saw it. Yes, there *was* somebody there, coming out of the shadow of the trees. And it was a boy.

The boy was not very tall. He was carrying a small bow – the sort used to shoot arrows

– and over his shoulder he had slung a bag made of brown animal skin. He was coming straight towards them, and he was singing, quite unaware of their presence.

Precious stepped forward and greeted him in Setswana, which is the language many people speak in Botswana.

The boy stopped in his tracks. Then, in a sudden movement he dropped to his

haunches, whipped an arrow out of the quiver dangling from his belt and pointed the weapon at them.

Precious raised a hand in greeting. "Don't be frightened," she said. "It's just my friend and me. We're lost."

The boy stared at them. He must have realised they meant him no harm, for he straightened up and lowered his bow and arrow. Then, very slowly, he advanced towards them.

"Do you know how to get to the village near here?" Precious asked.

The boy looked at her and frowned.

"The village?" Precious repeated.

Nancy had been watching closely. Now she understood. "He doesn't understand," she said. "He doesn't speak our language."

Suddenly the boy spoke. It sounded

strange to them, as he used speech that was half whistle, half words. It was like hearing a bird speaking.

The moment he opened his mouth, Precious knew: this boy was a member of a group of people called the San. They were people who had lived in and around the Kalahari Desert for a long time. They were expert hunters and knew all there was to know about that dry and beautiful place. But how could she communicate with this boy, who had no idea of who they were or where they were going?

Suddenly it came to her. Tapping the boy lightly on the shoulder, she pointed to the ground beneath their feet. She dropped to her knees and began to draw in the sand. She drew a village, with huts and paths. She drew a cattle pen of the sort she knew villages in that part of the country always had next to them. She drew people standing round the huts.

The boy watched very carefully. Then,

jabbing at the picture with a finger, he said something more. But once again neither Precious nor Nancy could make out what it was.

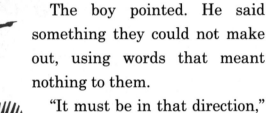

The boy pointed. He said something they could not make out, using words that meant nothing to them.

"It must be in that direction," said Nancy. "He's showing us."

The boy stood up straight and pointed again. He was looking at Precious as if puzzled as to why she could not understand what he was saying. Then he began to move off, gesturing to them to follow him.

They had wandered further than they had imagined, as they now began a walk that lasted many hours. As the sun began to sink below the horizon, it turned the sky deep red, as if the clouds were on fire. Then, as quickly as the sky had come ablaze, the red turned to dark blue, dotted with tiny points of silver light from thousands and

thousands of stars.

Precious made sure she stayed close to the boy, and that Nancy stayed at her side. She did not want to get lost again. She did not want to be wandering around in a place like this, so far from anywhere, so lonely, so dangerous for any unfortunate creatures on their own.

After a couple of hours, the boy signalled for them to stop. He pointed ahead and gestured to the girls to crouch down behind him.

"What is it?" whispered Nancy, her voice wavering with fear.

"I don't know," answered Precious. "He's seen something."

In the silence of the night, at first it seemed to Precious that the only sound was that of her heart hammering within her. But then another sound caught her attention – the sound of something moving in the bush, something crashing through vegetation.

She sensed immediately that it must be a big creature. Most animals move quite silently, but the bigger ones – elephants, buffalos or rhinos – barge through the undergrowth not caring what they knock down or flatten. The noise she heard definitely came from something big.

She tried to make out shapes in the darkness, but there was no moon, and the stars gave out only a very faint light. She could see the trees, of course, but there was no way of telling what the shapes beneath them were. Until one of them moved – and then she knew. An elephant ... Another shape moved. Two elephants.

Precious knew they were in real danger. Elephants do not like people to get too close to them, and if they do so, they will often charge. If you are charged by an elephant, your only hope is that it will decide not to

bother to carry through with its attack. If it does decide to see the charge through, then nothing can save you.

The boy reached for Precious's hand and began to lead her and Nancy very slowly off to one side. They crept along as silently as they could, hoping that the elephants would not hear them, and they might have succeeded had Nancy not trodden on a large twig. Under her weight the twig broke with a crack that sounded as loud as a pistol shot.

There was a flurry of activity from the elephants. This came along with a trumpeting

64

– a sort of challenge – from one of them. The boy seized Precious by the arm and pulled her behind him. Nancy clung on to Precious's hand, and the three of them ran as fast as they could through a bed of reeds away from the elephants.

It could all have ended very badly, but fortunately it did not. The elephants decided that whatever had made the noise was no threat and had gone away. They resumed their browsing.

The three children continued. Precious and Nancy were now rather tired and were finding it difficult to keep up with the boy, but they knew that they could not lag behind again. For his part, the boy sensed their exhaustion and stopped to dig up the root of a wild plant. Taking a knife from his quiver, he cut it into several parts and offered it to the girls. He gestured to them to eat.

The root tasted delicious, and because it was so moist it quenched their thirst. But it also seemed to give them the energy to continue, and when they set off on their way again they had no difficulty in keeping up with their young guide.

It was deep into the night when they saw a few lights in the distance. These were lamps from the village, and meant that they were safe.

"We've made it," said Precious.

"Yes," said Nancy. "Thanks to our new friend."

People in the village were still awake. Earlier on they had sent out search parties after the nurse had arrived and told them she had become separated from the two girls. These search parties had just returned, only to find that the very people they were looking for had now turned up. Everybody was most relieved.

Obed Ramotswe's cousin was most relieved of all.

"I was very, very worried," he said. "The bush is dangerous at night."

Precious struggled to keep her eyes open. She was extremely tired. "Well, we're here now," she said. "Thanks to this ..."

She turned to point to the boy, but he had vanished.

"There was a boy!" she said.

The cousin nodded. "I saw him," he said. "That was a little San boy. His people live out there. They know how to survive in the bush."

"I didn't have time to thank him," said Precious. "I wanted to tell him how grateful we feel."

"Don't worry," the cousin reassured her. "I think he knows."

They spoke to the nurse. She had spent hours worrying about them and was crying with relief that they had been found. Then they went off with the cousin and his wife to sleep at their house. They were given a small room with two comfortable sleeping mats, and were offered food. They were too tired to eat, though, and dropped straight off to sleep the moment they lay down.

Precious had vivid dreams that night. There were elephants, and shapes that might have been elephants. There were strange birds. There was a little boy with a bow and arrows. There was her father, smiling at her, saying, *You must be more careful, my darling.* And in one of her dreams, an elephant said something to her, but it was in elephant language and she could not understand it. So she simply waved to it and the elephant waved back with its trunk before it became a shadow again and disappeared.

THE NEXT MORNING they had a large breakfast with the cousin and the cousin's wife and children. The cousin had three children, one of whom was the same age as Precious. They had never met before, even if they were distant cousins, and it was very exciting to discover and meet a new relative. After breakfast, as they sat in front of the house, enjoying the warm morning sun, Nancy told the cousin about how she had come to own the necklace and the photograph.

When she had finished, the cousin's wife

sighed. "That is a very sad story," she said. "Can you show me these things?"

The photograph was passed over, and then the zebra necklace.

"My father said that these hills are near this place," said Precious. "Is that true?"

The cousin's wife peered more closely at the photograph. "Yes," she said, looking up at Precious. "Those are our hills. They are only two or three miles away. Those are definitely our hills."

Precious gave Nancy a nudge. "You see,"

she whispered. "We are in the right place."

Now she asked the really important question. "Do you know who that lady is?" she enquired.

The cousin's wife looked at the photograph again. She passed it on to her husband, who also examined it closely. They both shook their heads, which made the girls' hearts sink.

"I'm afraid not," said the cousin. "We do not know that person."

Precious pointed to the necklace. "That

is something that belonged to her," she said. "That was her necklace."

The cousin's wife took the necklace in her hand and felt the smooth carved beads. "Zebras," she muttered. "They are very pretty creatures."

"Have you ever seen it before?" asked Precious.

The cousin's wife shook her head again. But then she said something that made both girls sit up straight. "I haven't seen this particular necklace," said the cousin's wife. "But I know the woman who makes them."

This was a very important clue, and Precious Ramotswe, as a budding detective, was very interested in clues. "Who is this lady?" she asked.

"She lives on the edge of the village," she said. "She is a very old woman now, and she doesn't make these necklaces any more. But this is clearly her work."

Precious turned to Nancy, who was shivering with excitement. "Perhaps that lady will remember your mother," she said.

"I can take you to see her," said the cousin's wife. "I know her well, and she will be very happy to see you. She doesn't get many visitors, you see, and when you don't get many people coming to see you, then there is always a welcome for anyone. "

They found the old woman sitting outside her house. When she saw them approaching, she clapped her hands together, greeting them with a broad smile that was almost entirely toothless.

"You are very welcome, girls," she said. "Tell me: where have you come from?"

Precious and Nancy told her about Mochudi, the village in which they both went to school. As they spoke, the old woman nodded to show that she liked what she was hearing. "It sounds like a very fine place," she said. "I have never been anywhere else, but if I ever do go somewhere, then I shall certainly go to Mochudi."

The cousin now raised the subject of the necklace. "This girl," she said, gesturing to

Nancy, "has a necklace she would like to show to you."

At a signal from the cousin, Nancy took the zebra necklace out of her pocket and handed it over. The old woman took it, her eyes shining with pleasure. "But I remember this," she exclaimed. "This is the best necklace I ever made. It took me a very long time."

"Do you remember who you sold it to?" Precious asked.

For a moment she feared that the old woman would shake her head and say no, but she did not. Instead there came a very unexpected answer. "Of course I remember," she said. "I made it for my own daughter. I gave it to her because she loved zebras."

There was silence. *I made it for my own daughter ...*

Precious saw that Nancy was shaking. She reached out and took her hand. Then she turned to face the old woman again.

"Do you think she may have given it away?"

The old woman looked indignant. "Of course not. She kept it."

Precious wanted to know a bit more. "What happened to her?" she asked.

The old woman's face clouded over. "It is not a happy story. She went away and was married to a man I never met, because they lived so far away. They had a child – a daughter. They called her Nancy. I never met her either. Then something terrible happened."

They waited. Nancy was looking at the ground; she was not sure she wanted to hear of this terrible thing. But the old woman seemed determined to continue. "They were accused of cattle theft. They went to prison for four years for stealing cattle. The girl went to live with other people, and her mother and father never saw her again. The girl was looked after by these kind people, but they moved away and nobody knew

where they had gone. I think the parents were ashamed too and might have thought it better for the girl to be with those people. They were ashamed, you see, about being sent to prison, even though they said they never stole those cattle. And I believe them, by the way." She paused. "You see, I did tell you it was going to be sad."

"And the girl?" Precious asked.

"I have no idea," came the answer.

"I think I know the answer to that," said Nancy.

Precious remained quiet. She had never imagined that this would happen. Nancy had found the answer to her quest – but would she ever have thought that it would be this? Precious looked enquiringly at Nancy, wondering what she would say.

"I am that girl," said Nancy. She did not say this in a loud voice; she spoke softly, but loud enough for the old woman to hear her perfectly well.

The old woman blinked. Then she looked up at the sky, as if she were struggling to find words and might find some up there.

"You are that girl ..." The old woman said, so softly as if to be talking to herself. "You are that girl."

"Yes," said Nancy. "I think I am. That necklace was my mother's. And my name is —"

"Nancy," whispered the old woman.

"Yes."

The old woman let out a wail of joy. Then, rather unsteady on her feet, she stood up and folded Nancy in her arms. "You are my granddaughter," she whispered. "And now you have come to me."

The old woman began to cry – not tears of sorrow, but tears of joy. Nancy cried too – the same sort of tears that were being shed by her grandmother. For we do not only cry when we are sad; we can cry when our hearts are so full of joy and happiness that there are no words to show how we feel – and it is left to tears to do that.

That was not the end of the story of the zebra necklace. Precious had found Nancy's grandmother for her, but the search did not end there. The two girls went home with the nurse the next day. On the way back to the car they stayed very close to one another, of course, as there are some mistakes you do not want to make twice.

The old woman had told them where Nancy's parents now lived. It was not far from Mochudi, and so Precious was able to ask her father to take them there a few days later. Nancy had spoken to the people who looked after her and had told them the full story. They were pleased with what had happened.

"You always have a home with us, you know," they said. "But it is important for you to find your parents, and we are happy that this will now happen. And if you want to live with them, then we shall understand."

Obed Ramotswe drove them there in his truck. It was only half an hour away, along quite a good road, with no bumps – and no elephants either. When they arrived, Precious said that she would sit in the

car with her father while Nancy knocked
on the door of the house. But that was not
what Nancy wanted.

"You are the one who solved this
mystery," she said. "That's why I want you
to come with me – and your father too."

So it was that the three of them stood
outside the small house that morning and
knocked on the door. It was only three
knocks – *knock, knock, knock* – but Precious
knew that for Nancy knocking on that door
was the most important thing she had ever
done in her life.

A woman came to the door. She looked surprised to see visitors, and it was obvious that she had no idea who was standing before her. Then a man appeared behind her and peered at the visitors too. Both the man and the woman had kind faces.

Nancy opened her mouth to speak, but she closed it again before any words came. Reaching into a bag she had brought with her, she took out the necklace and held it out before her.

The woman stared at the necklace for a full few minutes. Then her gaze moved up and fell on Nancy. She knew.

In Botswana there is an old custom. If you are very, very happy – not just happy in the ordinary, everyday way, but much happier than that – you show your happiness by making a lovely *wooh* sound. You repeat it – like this: *WOOH! WOOH! WOOH!*

That is the sound the woman made, right there on the doorstep. Then she rushed

forward and hugged Nancy so tightly that
Precious thought her friend would disappear
altogether. Love can do that, you know – it
can make you disappear. That is because
love can cover everything, including things
that are sad. So love – and kindness – can
cover up hate and unkindness and make
them go away. It can do all of that – and
more.

Everything worked out well for Nancy.

Her parents were overjoyed that they had
been united again with their daughter, and
Nancy, of course, was very happy to have
found them. From that day onwards, she
stayed with them, although she often spent
the weekends, and the occasional weekday,

with the kind people who had looked after her all that time. "I am very lucky," she said. "I am a girl with four parents!"

Precious was happy, too. It was one of her best cases, she thought, and later, when she grew up and became one of the best private detectives in Botswana, she always remembered how well it had turned out.

And there is one more thing. To thank Precious for the help she had given them, Nancy and her newly found family gave her a special present. You have probably guessed what it was. Yes, a zebra necklace, specially made by the grandmother. It was beautifully crafted, of course, as is anything that is made with love.

Other books in this series featuring
Precious Ramotswe, available in
print and eBook, are:

Precious and the Monkeys

Precious and the Mystery of Meerkat Hill

*Precious and the Mystery of
the Missing Lion*